Myth

5 $\frac{50}{si}$

$12/2$

hawaiian myths of earth, sea, and sky

hawaiian myths of

illustrated by marilyn kahalewai

EARTH, SEA, AND SKY

VIVIAN L. THOMPSON

A Kolowalu Book
University of Hawaii Press
Honolulu

03   02   01   00   99   98   10   9   8   7   6

Designed by Helen Gentry

Library of Congress Cataloging-in-Publication Data

Thompson, Vivian Laubach.
   Hawaiian myths of earth, sea, and sky/by Vivian L. Thompson; illustrated by Marilyn Kahalewai.
      p.   cm.
   Originally published: New York: Holiday House, 1966.
   Bibliography: p.
   Summary: Presents twelve Hawaiian myths which explain how the earth was created, why volcanoes on Hawaii erupt, why the days are longer in summer, and other natural phenomena.
   ISBN 0-8248-1171-2
   1. Mythology, Hawaiian. [1. Mythology, Hawaiian.] I. Title.
BL2630.H38T46 1988   88-1325
299'.92—dc19   CIP
                                           AC

University of Hawai'i Press books are printed on acid-free paper and meet the guidelines for permanence and durability of the Council on Library Resources

To Jackie Johnson Debus
because this book marked
the beginning of a treasured
friendship

CONTENTS

PREFACE

FAR OUT IN THE BLUE PACIFIC, a volcanic mountain range rises from the ocean floor to form the group of islands called Hawaii. To these islands long, long ago, in great double canoes, came the Polynesians (people from many islands). They called this place "Hawaii-with-the-green-back." It was warmed by tropic sun, cooled by trade winds, washed by misty rains.

The Polynesians made these islands their new home. Mild evenings, by the light of the candlenut torches, they gathered to listen to their story tellers.

At first they heard only the stories brought from their former island homes. These were myths of gods who made earth, sea, and sky; of mo-o, terrifying monster lizards; of kupua, part-man and part-god, with superhuman gifts and the ability to change form into animal or plant, stone or fog.

In time the Hawaiians began to tell stories about their new home, to explain the natural wonders they found there. They imagined beautiful goddesses in the volcano, in the snow-capped mountains, in the moon; heroes who captured the sun, tossed the chief of sharks into the sky, and broke the mighty surf into harmless little waves. They tried to account for sudden storms, odd rock formations, man-eating sharks, and all the bewildering aspects of their new world of islands.

Here are some of those stories—a small part of the rich heritage which we have from Hawaii. If the Hawaiian words seem strange, the glossary at the back of the book will be helpful.

ACKNOWLEDGEMENT

To the many people who helped me locate source material and check the manuscript for accuracy, my warm Mahalo nui loa.

My special thanks to Nona Beamer; Edwin H. Bryan Jr., Pacific Scientific Information Center, Bishop Museum; Yasuto Kaihara, Hawaiian-Pacific Collection, University of Hawaii Library, Honolulu; David Kittelson, University of Hawaii Library, Hilo; Lucille McMahon; Margaret Shipman; Malia Solomon, Ulu Mau Village; Bill Sproat; Helen Willocks and Staff of Hawaii County Library, Hilo.

hawaiian myths of earth, sea, and sky

The Time of Deep Darkness

In the Time of Deep Darkness, before the memory of man, the great gods Kane, Ku, Lono, and Kanaloa, came out of the night . . . .

KANE, GOD OF CREATION, picked up a vast calabash floating in the sea, and tossed it high into the air. Its top flew off and became the curved bowl, sky. Two great pieces of the calabash broke away; one became the sun, the other the moon. The seeds scattered and became stars. The remainder of the calabash became the earth and fell back into the sea.

Kane said, "I shall make a chief to rule the earth. Let us provide for his needs."

Kanaloa, god of the vast, endless sea said, "I shall fill the waters with living things—sea creatures for the chief's use." This he did.

> Born was the coral, born was the coral,
> Born was the starfish,
> Born was the conch shell;
> Born was the fish,
> Born was the porpoise,
> Born was the shark in the sea there swimming.

Kane said, "I shall fill the earth with living things: flyers and crawlers, slow-movers and swift-movers; land creatures for the chief's use." This he did.

> Born was the caterpillar, the parent;
> Out came the child, a moth, and flew.
> Born was the egg, the parent;
> Out came its child, the bird, and flew.
> Land birds were born,
> Sea birds were born,
> Birds that fly in a flock,
> Shutting out the sun.
>
> The sea crept up to the land,
> Crept backward, crept forward,
> Producing the family of crawlers:
> The rough-backed turtles,
> The sleek-skinned geckos,
> Mud-dwellers and track-leavers.

Ku, god of forests, said, "I shall cause trees to grow; trees to give wood for the chief's use." This he did.

> Thick grew the forests: koa and candlenut;
> Thick grew the forests: hau, wiliwili.
> Koa for paddles,
> Hau for lashings,
> Soft wiliwili for outrigger floats;
> Woods for the chief's canoe, swift as an arrow.
> Candlenut torches, to light the chief's way.

Lono, god of growing things, said, "I shall cause food plants to grow; food for the chief." This he did.

> Green blades came sprouting:
> Coconut, breadfruit, sweet potato, sugar cane,
> Taro, banana, arrowroot, yam.

When all was ready Kane said to Ku, Lono, and Kanaloa, "Now it is time. Go, find what is needed to make a chief."

To the north and west, to the south and east went the gods. On the sunrise side of a hill near the sea they found rich red earth. This they took to Kane, who made the figure of a man and breathed life into it. The man walked about and spoke, and the gods were pleased.

Kane said, "We shall call him Red Earth Man."

Red Earth Man was happy. Soon he saw that wherever he went something went with him. It walked when he walked, and rested when he rested. He was pleased to have company, and he called this thing Ke Aka, or shadow. He talked to it, he laughed at it, and sometimes he even sang to it. But Ke Aka never answered.

After a time the songs of Red Earth Man stopped. His laughter died away, and he no longer spoke. The gods saw that he was lonely.

"He needs a living companion," said Kane.

While Red Earth Man slept Kane breathed life into Ke Aka.

When Red Earth Man woke he stretched and looked about. "It is a fine day," he said aloud.

"A fine day indeed," a voice at his side agreed.

Red Earth Man was startled. "Ke Aka, you speak!"

Ke Aka nodded, smiling. Then Red Earth Man laughed, and his laughter was good to hear. He sang, and Ke Aka sang with him. Their song was so beautiful that the birds flew down to listen.

Red Earth Man said, "You were my shadow but now you are alive! I shall call you Living Shadow."

Then Red Earth Man and Living Shadow knelt and touched their heads to earth, to give thanks to the great gods for the gifts of life and companionship.

> In time, men multiplied.
> In time, men came from afar.
> Born were the fair-haired,
> Born the dark-haired.
> Born were the broad-chested,
> Born the big eaters.
> Born were the song-chanters,
> Born the family men.
> Born were war leaders,
> Born the high chiefs of long life.
> Ever increasing in number, men spread abroad.
> Man was here now; it was DAY.

A BATTLE NOBODY WON

Dead craters stand black and cold on the islands of Kauai, Oahu, and Maui. Only on the island of Hawaii do living volcanoes smoke and seethe. There in the crater of Great Kilauea the volcano goddess Pele makes her home . . . .

ON FLOATING ISLAND lived a large family of brothers and sisters who were gods. Each one had a special power, but none was as powerful as the four great gods of creation.

This family was ruled by the eldest brother Ka Moho, the god of steam. His brothers were gods of thunder, earth-shaking, and fire-keeping. His sisters were goddesses of sea, volcano, lightning, and clouds.

Pele, a handsome young woman with a back straight as a cliff, was Volcano Goddess. Steam God ordered Fire-Keeper God to teach Pele all his secrets of fire-making. When she had learned them, he gave her a magic spade and fire sticks and she dug her first fire pit.

Red-gold lava bubbled up, overflowed the pit, and ran down to the sea. Pele watched, fascinated, but Namaka, Sea Goddess, was furious. The lava killed hundreds of fish. She went to Ka Moho, the god of steam, and demanded that Pele be punished.

Steam God called a family council. He looked at the angry faces of the two sisters and knew there could never be peace between them. Then he spoke.

"Pele, it is best that you go forth and find a home of your own. Brothers, get her a fine strong canoe. You, Namaka, lend her your two servants, Tide and Current, to be her canoe helpers."

The brothers agreed willingly, and the sister sullenly.

Pele said to Namaka, "Soon, dear sister, you shall see my fiery cloud rising from an island where I am the ruler—I, alone!"

Namaka, about to make an angry reply, was interrupted by the youngest sister, Hiiaka, the goddess of lightning. "Let me go with you, Pele!" she cried.

Ka Moho shook his head. "When Pele has found a home, she may send for you."

So it was decided and so it was done. Pele, carrying her fire sticks and magic spade, bid her family farewell, and stepped into the canoe. Tide and Current pushed the canoe out to sea.

Day followed day, and night followed night. The canoe came to a chain of islands. At Kauai, Pele ordered her helpers to land. There, with her magic spade, Volcano Goddess dug a pit and kindled a blaze. A cloud of smoke arose, making a dark smudge in the sky.

From Floating Island, Namaka saw the smoke and remembered Pele's words. Spitefully, Sea Goddess sent waves rolling across the water and drowned the fire.

Pele ordered Tide and Current to take her to the larger island of Oahu. There in several places she dug pits and started fires, sending clouds of sulphur smoke billowing upward.

When Namaka saw these, she churned up a great storm and lashed the island of Oahu with sheets of rain until the last spark of Pele's fire sputtered and died.

Pele ordered Tide and Current on, to the island of Maui. There she climbed a high mountain and dug deep. Soon fiery fountains leaped high, spreading a red glare across the sky.

This time Namaka decided to go herself and destroy Pele. She rode her sea monster and skimmed across the waters to the Maui shore. Climbing the mountain, she saw Pele on the western slope.

There the two goddesses, Sea and Volcano, met and fought. Each goddess used every trick she knew with water or with fire. For days, on and on, the battle raged. Finally, Sea drowned the last of Volcano's fires and returned home.

But Namaka had not drowned Pele.

Pele soon found her fire sticks and magic spade and returned to her canoe. She looked across the water and saw, hanging above the island of Hawaii, a mantle of smoke. It was not of her making. Curious, she ordered Tide and Current to take her there.

When Pele landed, at the Place-of-Quiet-Burning, she saw

that the smoke came from the crater called Great Kilauea. This was the home of a fire god, Forest-Eater. His appetite was so huge nothing could satisfy it. He devoured trees, crops, houses, people.

Pele had heard that no one but his small white dog dared approach him. She smiled—Pele dared approach him! If she joined Forest-Eater that should put an end to Namaka's trouble-making.

Up the mountain slope, along a chain of craters, went Pele. Though she found spatter cones and steaming cracks, she caught no glimpse of Forest-Eater.

She reached Little Kilauea. Still no sign of Forest-Eater. She came at last to Great Kilauea and there, at the edge of the huge pit, sat a small white dog, howling mournfully. Of Forest-Eater there was no trace.

Pele searched for days without success. Then she settled down in Forest-Eater's home and sent Tide and Current back for her sister Hiiaka, the goddess of lightning.

Namaka, convinced at last that she could never destroy Pele, decided to ignore her.

No one ever saw Forest-Eater again. Some say that he moved to an unknown island rather than share his crater home with the volcano goddess. Others say he simply ate himself to death.

In time, even his dog stopped looking for him and became Pele's follower. Sometimes this small white dog is seen running across the bleak lava fields. Sometimes people tell of meeting Pele on the lonely roads near Kilauea.

If the volcano remains quiet, people know that Volcano Goddess is pleased with those she met. But if the earth trembles, they know that someone has roused her anger, and there will soon be another eruption.

SPEARS OF LIGHTNING

Demon-terrors lurked in the dark places of the island of Hawaii. It came about that Hiiaka, the goddess of lightning, had to fight them with her weapon of light . . . .

THE YOUNG HIIAKA, left behind on Floating Island of the gods, was happy when the canoe returned and took her to join her sister Pele. The vast crater, Kilauea, filled Hiiaka with awe, but the change in Pele saddened her. The goddess of the volcano had become a cruel, hot-tempered ruler. So Hiiaka did not live with her, but in the district of Puna below Kilauea.

Her home was in a beautiful grove of lehua, the Tree-of-Fire-Bloom, that sprang up wherever the lava flows cooled. Here she met Hopoe, a graceful dancer, and the two became close friends. Together they made leis, or garlands, of feathery red lehua blossoms. Together they danced the sacred hulas.

As the goddess of lightning, Hiiaka was equal in rank to her sister but, even so, the goddess of the volcano gave orders to her. Before long Pele told Hiiaka to carry a message to the far end of the island. Hiiaka had no wish for such a journey. Yet how could she refuse? She had begged Pele to bring her to Hawaii.

To her friend, Hopoe, the news was frightening. "This is a dangerous journey, Hiiaka!" she said. "Many demons lie hidden in the shadows of forest, river, sea, and mountain. Let me go with you!"

Hiaaka shook her head. "Pele has ordered Fern Maiden to be my companion. I shall not be gone long. I must return before Moon is born new again. Such is my sister's command."

Hopoe took off the lehua lei she wore and placed it about Hiiaka's neck.

The young goddess smiled. "Do not be sad, Hopoe. Soon I shall dance again to the beat of your hula drum."

"May it be so," Hopoe answered.

"It will be so," said Hiiaka. "Pele has promised to protect you and these lehua groves until I return."

MOON still hung in the sky next morning, when Hiiaka rose. She put on her skirt of leaves and wrapped her magic pa-u about her, drawing the loose end up over her shoulder.

She and Fern Maiden set out. At the edge of a forest they met a young woman named Singing Thrush, who lived on the far side. She told them of Forest Demon who haunted these woods, and offered to guide them through.

As she led them into the forest gloom, chilling fog closed about them. Unseen roots tripped them. Thorny vines clawed at them. Sharp-billed birds darted at them.

"Fog, roots, vines, birds—all are Forest Demon's helpers," Singing Thrush said.

Ahead, a giant candlenut tree thrust its twisted branches toward them.

"That is no true tree!" Singing Thrush warned.

Fern Maiden cried, "Let us go back!"

Hiiaka said, "No. We shall go on."

"Not so!" roared a terrible voice.

Through the drifting fog, a writhing shape came toward them. Lightning Goddess snatched off her pa-u and whirled it. A flash lighted the dark forest, and they saw the fearsome demon.

Lightning Goddess whirled her pa-u again. Lightning spears cut into Forest Demon and he died. The three young women passed safely through the woods.

M O O N was rising and slender.

The three young women spent the night at Singing Thrush's home. She wished to go on with them next morning, and Hiiaka consented.

As Moon paled they were on their way. Before noon they came to a rushing river. At the crossing place two rough logs stretched

to the far shore. On a rock near the water travelers were placing gifts of fish, coconut, and fruits.

One said to Hiiaka, "If you would cross safely, make a large offering to Lizard Women."

The three maidens watched another traveler—an old woman—place a small offering on the rock. She hobbled to the crossing logs. As she set foot upon one of them, it curled up and seized her.

Hiiaka saw that the logs were tongues—the tongues of two monstrous creatures with witch heads and giant lizard bodies; Lizard Women. She pulled the old woman to safety. Lizard Women, with tongues and tails, then tried to drag Hiiaka into the churning water. The goddess whirled her pa-u. Lightning spears struck Lizard Women and turned them to stone.

The grateful travelers gave their food gifts to the goddess, and she and her companions went on their way.

T H R O U G H the growing large of Moon—eight nights and days—their path lay along the top of a seacoast cliff.

Fern Maiden's skill in finding food and shelter eased their weariness. Singing Thrush's songs kept up their spirits. But each night, as Hiiaka saw Moon grow larger, she wondered what her hot-tempered sister might do if she returned late.

One day their path ended, cut off by a wide break in the cliff. Below the sea surged and pounded. On the far side of this watery gap they saw their trail continue. Carefully they made their way down to a rocky shelf overlooking the sea.

"The day is warm, and the water inviting," said Fern Maiden.

"O Hiiaka, let us swim across," said Singing Thrush.

"Wait!" commanded the goddess. She broke a branch from a bush and tossed it down. The water swirled. The branch vanished in a flash of spray.

"Only a trick of the current," Singing Thrush said, and made ready to dive.

"Not so!" said Hiiaka. She dropped a cluster of leaves in a different spot. The ugly head of Man-Eater Shark rose from the water and snatched the leaves.

Lightning Goddess and the shark fought. He churned up waves powerful enough to sweep the women from their ledge. Fern Maiden and Singing Thrush drew back. The goddess hurled her spears of lightning into Man-Eater Shark until his lifeless body sank from sight.

M O O N ' S sharp horns were growing round. As Hiiaka looked at them that night, she knew her time was already one-third gone.

On they went until they came to mountains. There they met a young chief, who gave them food and shelter. He told them that his district was plagued by many mo-o. The chief and his warriors led the travelers on their way, up the winding trail of the mo-o. On one side the mountain stood, pitted with dark caves. On the other, the land dropped sharply away to a plain, far below.

Without warning, a gigantic lizard-like beast with mighty legs sprang from one of the dark caves. It was Great Mo-o. The chief and his men attacked him with their sharp spears. These did not pierce the tough hide. Angered, Great Mo-o sprang again. His lashing tail struck Fern Maiden to the ground. Singing Thrush knelt to care for her.

Lightning Goddess fought beside the warriors, hurling her lightning spears until Great Mo-o dropped in the trail, dying. The chief's men dragged the ugly body to the cliffside and flung it over.

Then from the cave swarmed hundreds of little mo-o: They sprang great distances. Warriors struck at the leaping creatures with war clubs, but each time one was killed, two more sprang to take his place.

Lightning Goddess began to call upon her brother and sister gods of the storm. She split the sky with lightning and flashed light into the dark caves. A mighty rain fell, sweeping the hordes of little mo-o to death on the plain below.

MOON had reached its roundness. There was no time to lose. Hiiaka left Fern Maiden with the chief's people to recover, while she and Singing Thrush finished their journey. They traveled swiftly to the seacoast, delivered Pele's message, and returned.

The young chief told them he wished to marry Fern Maiden and Hiiaka gave her consent. He gave a great feast in honor of the goddess, to thank her for helping to rid his district of the mo-o.

MOON was moving to smallness as Hiiaka and Singing Thrush began their return journey. As they left the mountains of the mo-o behind, Moon showed sharp horns again. As they passed the sea of Man-Eater Shark, Moon grew weak and wasted. As they crossed the river of Lizard Women, Moon drew its last breath. When they reached the home of Singing Thrush, night-of-no-Moon was upon them.

"O Hiiaka," said Singing Thrush, "with your lightning spears you have rid the island of the darkness-terrors. Now our people may travel without fear. But tonight you must eat and rest."

Hiiaka hesitated. Moon would not be born again until the next night, but she wished to be home early. If she should be late, her fiery sister would show no mercy. Yet if she went on tonight, she might lose her way in the dark forest. She decided to stay.

MORNING Star still burned in the sky when Lightning Goddess and Singing Thrush parted. Hiiaka hurried on. Before mid-morning, sulphur smoke burned her nostrils. Kilauea lay beyond the next bend. She moved swiftly, then stopped.

Her lehua grove was a smoking ruin. Lava from the fire pit of Kilauea still flowed across it. The hot-tempered volcano goddess had broken her promise.

But Hiiaka saw Hopoe standing on a ledge. She was in the lava's path, and Hiiaka ran toward her, calling her name.

Hopoe moved a little but did not answer. When the lightning goddess reached the ledge, she knew her friend would never speak again. Pele, instead of protecting Hopoe, had turned her to stone —a stone that swayed with every breeze.

From that time on Hopoe was known as the Dancing-Stone-of-Puna.

A STRANGE SLED RACE

The goddess of snow, Poliahu, lives high on the slopes of Mauna Kea on the northern side of Hawaii. That side is free of lava flows because of the goddess's skill at sled-racing . . . .

POLIAHU AND HER SNOW maidens one day covered their dazzling snow mantles with mantles of golden sunshine. They took their long, slender sleds to the race course below the snowfields. There a narrow grassy track had been laid, dropping swiftly toward the sea.

High, tinkling laughter filled the air as the maidens urged the goddess to race. Poliahu was very willing. She made a running start, threw herself upon her sled, and plunged down. Far below she came to a stop, marked the spot, and lifted her sled aside.

One after another the snow maidens followed, but none reached the goddess's mark. As they gathered below they discovered a stranger in their midst, a handsome woman dressed in black mantle and robe.

Fixing gleaming black eyes upon the goddess of snow, she spoke. "I should like to race with you, but I have no sled."

"You may use one of ours," Snow Goddess said, and a maiden quickly offered hers.

The stranger took it without a word of thanks. Then she and Poliahu climbed up the mountain slope. The maidens watched from below. The stranger swooped down the slope and flashed past them. There was no doubt she was skillful. Poliahu followed and passed the other's stopping place.

"That sled did not fit me!" said the dark-eyed stranger.

A taller maiden offered her sled. Again the long, slow climb. Again the short, swift descent. Both sleds went farther than before, but Poliahu's still led.

"An inferior sled!" the woman said with scorn.

"We have no inferior sleds," Snow Goddess replied coldly. "Let us race again, and you shall take mine."

"I have always raced on a longer course," said the woman. "Let us go higher up the mountain. You shall race first this time."

They exchanged sleds and climbed to the snow line. The stranger waited until Poliahu had started down; then she stamped her foot. The earth trembled. A jagged crack split open across the lower part of the racing course.

The snow maidens, watching below, lost sight of their goddess as steam rose from the crack and formed a curtain. They ran up the slope.

For a moment, the steam cleared. They caught a glimpse of Poliahu racing toward the widening crack. The woman in black was close behind her, standing upright on her speeding sled. In horror they saw her black robe turn red and her eyes glow like burning coals. They knew now! She was Pele—Volcano Goddess!

She stamped again. They felt the molten lava come rumbling through underground passages in answer to her signal. It spurted out along the crack.

Swiftly the snow maidens raised their arms toward the snowy peaks and began to chant. The air grew chill as gray Cloud Goddesses gathered to aid Poliahu. They sent snow swirling down from the top of the mountain, hissing as it struck the heated earth. The spurting lava died.

Pele, in a fury, gave a crackling shout. The lava leaped up again, forming a row of fiery fountains directly ahead of Poliahu.

The snow maidens watched fearfully. There was no way that Poliahu could slow her sled nor turn it aside. She plunged through the wall of fire.

Her golden mantle burst into flame. Throwing it off and leaping from her sled, Snow Goddess stood robed in dazzling white. A red-gold river raced toward her from the fire fountains. On its crest rode Pele. Poliahu waited, unmoved.

Volcano Goddess burst through the flames without harm. She sprang from her sled to face the young woman who dared to defy her.

Snow Goddess swung her mantle in a wide arc. A blast of icy wind swept down the mountain. Her silvery hair and dazzling garments streamed out behind her.

Volcano Goddess shivered. The leaping fountains dwindled. The racing river slowed.

She screamed at the lava, "Swallow her up!"

But the lava fountains died. The lava river grew sluggish. Still deadly, it flowed to the very feet of Snow Goddess. She flung her arms wide. The river split in two, leaving her unharmed in the center. It made its way beyond her, moving slowly down to the sea. There it formed a long, flat point of land, known to this day as Leaf-of-Smooth-Lava.

Volcano Goddess stared, unable to believe what she saw. Her red mantle turned black again. Her glowing eyes dulled. Shivering with cold, she disappeared as mysteriously as she had come.

High, tinkling laughter filled the air once more as the snow goddess and her maidens picked up their sleds and returned to their snowy home.

Pele never again crossed over Mauna Kea to Poliahu's side of the island, although she still sent lava pouring down the southern side.

THE LOST SUN, MOON, AND STARS

When the rainy season comes there are days without sunlight, nights without moonlight or starlight. Ask old Hawaiians why this is so and they will tell you . . . .

ONCE, LONG AGO, when chiefs were nearly as powerful as the gods, a district was ruled by a chief known as Kahoa-the-Cruel.

From morning until night his overseers drove the people. "Take out the canoes! The chief must have fresh fish!"..."Take your digging sticks to the taro fields! The chief must have fresh poi!" ..."Take your axes to the forest! The chief must have a koa log for another war canoe!" Day after day, so it went.

33

In that district lived a young man whose name was Kana. One day as he and his younger brother Niheu helped to haul a canoe log, an overseer began beating an old man. Niheu struck the overseer, who fell dead.

The boys knew that Niheu would be killed, if caught, and ran up the mountain trail to the home of their grandmother, Uli-of-the-Uplands. Before they reached her door Sun was blotted out and thick gray clouds filled the sky.

There was no need to tell Uli what had happened. She knew, for she was a goddess of sorcery.

"Chief Kahoa has already heard of your deed," she said. "He has decided to punish our people by taking away Sun, Moon, and Stars. He knows we cannot live without them."

Niheu knew then that he must give himself up.

But Kana said, "If we bring back Sun, Moon, and Stars, our people will be saved and your life as well."

Uli spoke. "It will not be easy to find where Chief Kahoa has hidden them, for he lives in Place-of-Darkness. But there is one who may be able to tell you, my sister, Woman-Who-Walks-in-Darkness."

"Where can we find her?" asked Niheu.

Uli spoke again. "You must journey toward the place where Sun has always risen. The slanting rain will fall upon you, and the cold wind will pierce your bones. Keep going. At a black cliff jutting out into the sea, there you will find my sister's home."

"Shall we take weapons?" asked Kana.

"Have you forgotten the magic gift I once gave you?" Uli answered. "It is kupua power—greater than any weapon. Use it when the time comes. Now hurry, before all light is gone."

Kana and Niheu set out. The slanting rain fell upon them, and the cold wind pierced their bones, but they kept on. Niheu's teeth began to chatter and his body to shake with a chill.

At last he said, "You must go on without me, Kana."

Kana covered his brother with his cape and left him resting beneath a tree. Then he stumbled on through the growing darkness until he saw in the distance the black cliff. At the foot of it a small fire burned before a hut. There he found a blind woman sitting by the fire.

"Aloha, Woman-Who-Walks-in-Darkness. It is Kana, grandson of Uli-of-the-Uplands, who seeks your help."

The old woman turned toward the sound of his voice. "Welcome, Kana, son of Uli. What is it you seek?"

Kana told her. "Can you tell me where to look for the lost Sun, Moon, and Stars?"

Woman-Who-Walks-in-Darkness said, "I can indeed. Chief Kahoa lives at the top of this high cliff. In the cliff is a tunnel where Sun goes to rest each evening, and Moon each morning. In this tunnel Kahoa stores his treasures and keeps his servants imprisoned. That is where he has trapped Sun, Moon, and Stars. It is said there is a great white stone in the mouth of the tunnel."

"I shall find it," said Kana.

"You will never reach the place, Kana. The trail is closely guarded."

"I will not go by the trail," said Kana. "I have magic power from Uli to help me go up the cliff. Will you lead me to a spot beneath the chief's house?"

Woman-Who-Walks-in-Darkness wasted no time. She rubbed her finger across his arm. "Your skin—is it light?"

"Yes," said Kana.

"We must darken it then, or you will be discovered. Chief Kahoa's men have dark skin."

She took charcoal from the fire and ground it into powder. She crushed a candlenut until its oil ran out. Then she made a paste of the two, which Kana spread on his skin.

"Now we shall go. Take hold of my pa-u," she said.

Grasping a fold of her pa-u, Kana followed as she walked silently along the narrow strip of sand between cliff and sea. Not a gleam of moonlight, not a glimmer of starlight broke the blackness. At his right hand, Kana could hear the sea lapping at the shore. With his left hand, he could feel the rough walls of the cliff.

When they had gone some distance Woman-Who-Walks-in-Darkness stopped. "The house is above us," she whispered.

"Now I will use my magic power," said Kana.

He stretched himself, growing taller and thinner. He stretched more and more...up...up...up...until he was tall enough to step out upon the rocky ledge. Ahead he saw the chief's house, lighted by burning torches at the entrance. From inside came the sound of laughter and Chief Kahoa's boastful voice.

Kana shrank back to his normal size. He crept through the darkness, closer to the house. Beyond it he saw a faint blur of light and moved toward it. Just as he was close enough to see that it was a white stone, the chief came through his doorway. Kana stood frozen at the side of the path, glad of his darkened skin.

Chief Kahoa strode past, close enough to touch, and knelt before the great white stone. Then he raised it slowly and called into the opening beneath.

"Food!"

A steaming calabash appeared. He took it and shouted, "I shall be back for more. Make ready!" Replacing the stone, he took the calabash of food back to the house.

Kana had stretched himself thin as a spider web and had little strength left. He needed food. Silently he crept to the stone and lifted. It moved a little, showing a gleam of light, then fell back into place. Gathering all his remaining strength, Kana pulled at the stone. Slowly he lifted it to one side. Holding it with one hand, he reached down into the opening with the other.

A calabash of steamed fish and coconut was handed to him. He slid the stone into place and ate quickly, feeling strength flow into his body.

Footsteps sounded. Kana stepped back into the darkness, holding the empty calabash. Chief Kahoa strode past. Again he lifted the stone. Again his command rang out.

"My drinking gourd with the Water-of-Life!"

When this appeared, he took it and shouted, "I shall be back for my new treasures. Make ready!"

Kahoa replaced the stone and carried the water to the house.

Kana remembered his grandmother telling of this Water-of-Life. Drinking it would cure any illness and protect one from death. He must drink, and carry some to Niheu. Then both would be safe from the chief's anger.

Kana set the stone aside and reached down his empty calabash. He called down in a gruff voice as much like the chief's as he could make it, "More of the Water-of-Life! Fill the calabash!"

For a moment, nothing happened. Then he heard water gurgling into the calabash. He gulped several mouthfuls and set the bowl in a safe place.

Taking a deep breath, he called down, "Now my treasures!"

Into his hands were placed twinkling Stars. Kana tossed them into the sky, where they shone softly in the blackness. He reached down again. His hands brought up the silver globe, Moon. He flung Moon into the sky, where it gleamed with a lovely light.

With Moon and Stars in place, the night was no longer dark. Soon Chief Kahoa would be coming out to see why. Kana must get Sun quickly, and escape.

He plunged his hands down again. Instead of Sun, they brought up a white cock. Kana snorted. He set the cock aside.

This time his hand brought up the blazing ball, Sun. At the first ray of light the white cock stretched himself, flapped his wings, and crowed loud and clear.

There was no time to lose.

Kana tossed Sun into the sky, and the world was bathed in light. As he started to run, he heard from the chief's house the clatter of spears being taken from their racks.

Kahoa and his men streamed out. The men surrounded Kana, spears drawn, ready to kill him when the chief gave the word. Before Chief Kahoa could speak, he saw Kana's body begin to stretch. Finally it towered so high that the men reached only to his ankle bones. The chief knew, and his men knew, that only one with kupua power could act so. They all fled.

Kana picked up the calabash of the Water-of-Life, took one mighty step to the edge of the cliff, and another to the beach below. There he shrank to his normal size, and told Woman-Who-Walks-in-Darkness what he had done. Then he hurried back to Niheu, who still lay shivering. Raising his brother from the ground, Kana held the calabash to his lips. After a few swallows of the Water-of-Life, Niheu was well enough to return home.

Their people met them with shouts and glad cries. And now, when the rains come and the sky stays dark, it is only a brief reminder of Chief Kahoa's cruel power and how it was broken.

The shark in the Milky Way

On clear nights when the sky is filled with stars and people look up at the Milky Way, they see the Chief of Sharks, and remember how he got there . . . .

IN THE DAYS of his childhood Ka-ulu's brother, Ka-ehu, had been carried off by the king of Far Island. Ka-ulu decided that when he grew up he would search for his lost brother. As he grew, he became known as Ka-ulu-the-Strong. Tales of the great things he could do spread to all the islands, even to Far Island.

At last the day came for Ka-ulu to begin his search. Carrying his paddle of koa wood, he went down to the beach to his canoe and set out.

40

When the king heard that Ka-ulu was on his way to Far Island, he sent the first of his powerful guards, Great-Rolling-Surf, against him.

Ka-ulu saw Great-Rolling-Surf coming toward him and called out, "Surf, are you strong?"

"I am!" roared Great-Rolling-Surf. "Strong enough to swamp your canoe!"

Ka-ulu looked down at his hands and said, "Left hand and right hand, a rolling surf is troublesome. We must do something about this."

When Surf reached him, Ka-ulu took it in his strong hands and broke it into little waves. Then, whistling, he picked up his paddle and sent his canoe on its way.

When Ka-ulu reached the shore of Far Island, he found the king's second guard: Great-Stone-Man-with-Eight-Foreheads—a figure so tall that his head towered above the clouds.

Ka-ulu called up to him, "Ho, man of many foreheads! Are you strong?"

"I am!" thundered Great-Stone-Man. "Strong enough to grind you to bits!"

Ka-ulu looked down and said, "Left hand and right hand, this man has been standing too long. He must be weary. We must do something about this."

When Great-Stone-Man reached for him, Ka-ulu seized him with his strong hands and held him to the ground until grass and trees grew over him and there was nothing to be seen but a great stone mountain with eight hills. Then, whistling, Ka-ulu went on his way.

The king was puzzled when Great-Rolling-Surf and Great-

Stone-Man did not report. He sent his third guard, Great-Barking-Dog, to attack.

Ka-ulu saw the dog bounding toward him and called out, "Dog, are you strong?"

"I am!" snarled Great-Barking-Dog. "Strong enough to eat you!"

Ka-ulu looked down and said, "Left hand and right hand, great dogs are a bother. We must do something about this."

When Great-Barking-Dog leaped at him, Ka-ulu took firm hold of him with his strong hands and broke him into little pieces. Each piece became a small dog that ran off yelping in terror. Then, whistling, Ka-ulu went on his way.

When Great-Barking-Dog did not return, the king gave orders to his warriors to watch for Ka-ulu and kill him. They hid at the top of the mountain where the king lived. As Ka-ulu started climbing, they sent Great-Rock crashing down.

Ka-ulu saw it coming and called out, "Rock, are you strong?"

"I am!" rumbled Great-Rock. "Strong enough to crush you!"

Ka-ulu said, "Left hand and right hand, big rocks are a nuisance. We must do something about this."

When the rock bounded toward him, Ka-ulu reached out a forefinger and stopped it. Taking it in his strong hands, he broke it into a hundred pebbles and tossed them down the mountainside. Then, whistling, he climbed up toward the king's home.

The king had ordered his warriors to form a circle about him with drawn spears. But when Ka-ulu came in sight, the warriors were terrified. They ran off and left the king alone.

Ka-ulu walked up and placed his hands lightly around the king's throat.

"O King, are you strong?" he asked softly.

"Not very!" the king squeaked.

"Are you strong enough to tell me where to find my lost brother, Ka-ehu?"

"O yes, I am strong enough for that!" squealed the king. "Go down to the sea and ask Chief of Sharks."

Ka-ulu went down to the sea and called out, "Chief of Sharks, I have come to find my lost brother, Ka-ehu. Can you tell me where he is?"

"O yes," answered Chief of Sharks. "Your brother is inside of me. But there is room for two. Come in and join him."

"Thank you," said Ka-ulu, "but I think he would rather join me, out here."

Then Ka-ulu took hold of the great jaws of Chief of Sharks and pulled them apart. Out came Ka-ehu, whom the shark had swallowed whole.

"Come, my brother, let us go home," said Ka-ulu. "But first, we must do something about this."

With his strong hands he picked up Chief of Sharks and tossed him into the sky. There his body shattered into a million pieces.

Then Ka-ulu the Strong and Ka-ehu his brother who had been lost but now was found went home to Hawaii.

A KUPUA PLAYS TRICKS

Kamapuaa was part-human, part-god, and so had kupua power to change his form. He used his power for making mischief, and signs of his pranks remain to this day in the Islands . . . .

THE CHIEFESS OF KAHANA once sent runners through her district with a message. At every village gathering place, a runner stood and called out: "The Chiefess of Kahana offers a great reward to the young man who can uproot her koa tree."

The young men of the district gathered on the grounds of the chiefess. Each one tried to pull up the tree, and each gave up.

45

Then a handsome man in loincloth and cape of pigskin came forward. He grasped the trunk with both hands. The muscles of his arms and shoulders stood out like thick ropes. With one mighty heave he uprooted the koa tree.

The chiefess decided to make this handsome young stranger her chief. That was the reward she had planned. She sent her attendants to bring him to her.

They could not find the young man anywhere. But they did see, on the edge of the crowd, a brown striped pig. It ran into the fields, and they raced after it. As they were about to overtake the pig it disappeared. In its place stood a white spotted pig. As they reached that it changed into a great black pig with bristles on its back.

"That is a kupua!" said their leader. "Let us not harm it."

Returning to their chiefess, the men told her that it was surely Kamapuaa, the Pig-Man, who had uprooted her tree.

ANOTHER TIME, KAMAPUAA climbed up Kilauea where Pele, the goddess of the volcano, and her maidens were dancing. He stood for a while watching them float above the boiling bubbles of the lava lake and slip between the leaping fire fountains.

"Pele! A man is here!" cried one.

"Send a cloud of sulphur fumes down upon him!" Pele ordered.

"He is a stranger," the dancer said. "Should we..."

"Would you allow a stranger to watch our sacred fire dance?" The goddess herself sent a sulphur cloud swirling down.

It blotted Kamapuaa from their sight, and they went on dancing.

"Pele! He is coming up!" another dancer cried.

"Blind him with hot ashes!"

"But he is a young man...and handsome..."

Pele swept to the edge of the pit and looked down.

Kamapuaa was wearing a yellow loincloth and shoulder cape and looked handsome indeed. He gave a jaunty wave and kept climbing. The wind blew his cape back and, as he turned to catch it, Pele saw the row of stiff bristles growing from his spine.

"You fools!" she screamed at her dancers. "This is Kamapuaa. He has come to make trouble. Stir up the fires in the pit!"

"Aloha, Pele," Kamapuaa called. "Have you no welcome for a visitor?"

Pele called,

> "Greetings, Pig-Man.
> Man of the black bristles,
> Man of the grunting voice,
> Man of the ugly snout."

Kamapuaa called back,

> "Greetings, lovely Pele.
> Pele of the red eyes,
> Pele of the sharp tongue,
> Pele of the hot temper."

"Begone!" said Pele. "I alone rule this island."

"Perhaps you have ruled alone too long," Kamapuaa answered.

"Perhaps you need a strong chief. Marry me and we shall rule together."

Pele stamped her foot furiously. Red-hot lava splashed out of the fire pit and started down the mountainside.

"You have my answer," she called, turning to face Kamapuaa.

He was not there. Where he had stood she saw a patch of bristling grass that turned aside her lava.

Volcano Goddess stamped again. Earth split open and fresh lava poured out. The grass began to smoulder. Before it could burst into flame, it changed into a fierce black pig with ugly fangs —Kamapuaa.

He raced down the mountainside, the stream of lava following him. When he reached the sea he plunged in. The lava flowed in after him, and a cloud of steam arose.

Even the tough-skinned pig-man could not bear the heat of the water. Grunting with pain, Kamapuaa changed his form once more. He became a grunting fish with a snout like a pig—the humu-humu-nuku-nuku-a-puaa.

THE TRICK WHICH PLEASED Kamapuaa most was one which he played on Olopana, King of Oahu. The king had a great fondness for chicken baked in the earth oven, or imu. The finest hens raised on the island were brought to the royal hen roost and kept under special guard.

One night Kamapuaa slipped past the guards and made off with every hen. The chief guard, called before the king next day, reported that nothing had been seen but a black pig trotting off in the moonlight.

King Olopana knew then that only Pig-Man could have played such a trick. He called out four hundred warriors, armed them with short clubs, and ordered them to bring Kamapuaa to him, bound.

The warriors found Kamapuaa enjoying a fine chicken dinner and laid hold of him. He changed into a black pig with sharp tusks, and killed all the warriors except one which he spared to carry the news to the king.

Olopana then called out eight hundred warriors, armed them with short clubs and long spears, and ordered them to bring Kamapuaa to him, without fail.

The warriors soon overtook Kamapuaa, still in his pig form, and captured him.

When the procession returned in triumph, bearing Kamapuaa slung from their poles like any ordinary pig, Olopana was jubilant. He gave orders to prepare a great feast of roast pig for the following day. He ordered the eight hundred warriors to stand guard over Pig-Man until the imu was ready for baking him.

But right then Pig-Man disappeared before their eyes! The warriors felt blows from an unseen club. They battled the invisible kupua, but his blows dealt death. Soon all eight hundred of the king's warriors, save one, were stretched lifeless upon the ground.

Kamapuaa had escaped again.

This time, King Olopana ordered every man on the island of Oahu to search for the mischief-maker. Soon a fisherman reported that he had seen Kamapuaa, the man, in his great forty-foot canoe, off the windward shore.

Olopana called out twelve hundred warriors to man his fleet of war canoes, and ordered them to bring back Kamapuaa dead or alive.

The canoe men soon overtook him. When he saw them coming, he paddled without haste along the coast and turned up a stream that flowed into the sea from a valley. Kamapuaa's was a fast canoe, made from a sound koa log, and he was soon out of sight.

The warriors knew this valley. It ended abruptly at the foot of a steep cliff. High rock walls closed in one side; a plunging waterfall the other. The king's men smiled. This time, Kamapuaa was surely trapped.

The canoe men turned up the stream. The river bed grew narrower, the walls steeper. The men paddled faster.

The first canoe reached the end of the gorge. There were the rock walls. There was the waterfall. But where was Kamapuaa? He and his canoe were nowhere to be seen.

The waterfall had slowed to a trickle. Beside it, up the wall of the gorge, a deep groove was scraped in the rock—a groove the size and shape of Kamapuaa's canoe. Could Pig-Man have scaled that sheer wall, hauling his great canoe after him? Impossible!

But at the top of the wall they saw Kamapuaa's laughing face—and something else. Something that explained why the waterfall had slowed to a trickle. Kamapuaa's canoe was damming up the flow.

Then he broke the dam. Down came a plunging torrent, dashing the king's canoes against the rocky walls and drowning the warriors.

Chiefess, goddess, king—all have gone; but many believe that Kamapuaa lives on. For the humu-humu-nuku-nuku-a-puaa still

swims in Hawaiian waters, and who can be sure that this fish with a pig's snout is only a fish? Wild black pigs still plunge through the upland forest, and who is to say that one of them is not Kamapuaa, the Pig-Man? On the island of Oahu there is a deep gorge known as The Valley of the Leaky Canoe. Its rock wall carries the clear outline of a great canoe. Who could have hauled such a canoe up that steep wall? Who but Kamapuaa, the kupua who played tricks?

ThE GiFT OF ThE hAiRy ONE

Maikoha lived out his life as a humble farmer, but upon his death he became the guardian god of tapa-makers . . . .

COLD WIND SWEPT down the valley as Sun reached his western gate. Maikoha shivered in his rough cape and loin-cloth of woven leaves. He stretched his withered hands toward the small fire where bananas, breadfruit, and fish lay broiling on the hot coals. His thoughts turned back to the days when he was young and strong...

Then his friends called him The Hairy One. They admired his

hairy, muscular body and talked of his skill in foot-racing, wrestling, and diving. In the war games, when he swung his club, no man could stand up to him.

He had a beautiful wife and two daughters. When the first was born her mother had a dream. She saw her child kneeling before a strange tree whose small new leaves stirred in the breeze, so she named her Rustling Leaf. The second daughter was born with a mole on her forehead. This foretold a great gift to be shared with many, so she was named Gifted Worker.

In the house of Maikoha the family food bowls were never empty. He watched the seasons carefully and planted in bright moonlight on nights of good omen. So did his neighbors, but none had crops as fine as his. Each year when first-fruit offerings were made to Kane, the god of creation, and to Lono, the god of growing things, Maikoha's were the finest taro, the fattest sweet potatoes, the firmest gourds. With growing things he had a special way that seemed to his neighbors little short of magic. But Maikoha knew that his way with earth was a special power, and told no one.

Now he sighed. All that had been long ago, in his youth. His daughters were grown. His wife was dead and his own time to die was near. Before that happened he must tell his daughters his life-long secret: he was a kupua with power to change himself into plant form, but only upon death.

He watched his daughters carry their food to the women's eating-house. He put a bit of steaming fish into his eating bowl. He was growing weak and needed food but, lost in thought, he forgot to eat.

Maikoha was wondering what plant form he should choose.

What kind would benefit his people most? They had plants for food in plenty. They had woods for canoes and houseposts; woods for digging sticks, carrying poles, and pounding boards. They had a shrub that gave them rope, and vines that grew food and water bowls.

Slanting rain began to fall, and Maikoha shivered again. Woven leaves did not make warm clothing, yet that was all they had. There was no plant that gave them enough warmth. This was the kind he must choose! He set aside his food bowl and called Rustling Leaf and Gifted Worker.

"Listen, my daughters," Maikoha said. "Soon I must go down the narrow-stranded way of death. Bury me here beside our rushing stream. In death I will have kupua power to change into a tree. It will give you tapa—the beaten thing. From tapa you can make clothing...warmer than this." His voice faded.

"What is tapa?" asked Rustling Leaf.

"How can we make such clothing?" asked Gifted Worker.

Maikoha was growing faint. "...the beaten thing...water..." he whispered, then fell silent in death.

Sadly, his daughters carried out his wish. As Maikoha had foretold, a tree grew up beside the rushing stream. It stood there the next morning, a tree never before seen in their islands: its bark smooth, its leaves hairy. It was a paper mulberry tree. They could see that it was The Hairy One, and touched the leaves in awe.

Gifted Worker spoke. "These leaves are not long enough to braid or weave."

"Perhaps the bark—" said Rustling Leaf. She peeled off a strip. The inner side was smooth and clean. She rolled it around her finger, thoughtfully.

Both were thinking of his last words, "tapa—the beaten thing —water."

Village women, coming to comfort the sisters, saw the strange tree. When they heard its story they dropped to their knees and touched their heads to the ground.

They whispered to each other, "Aia! Aia! The Hairy One lives on in this sacred tree!"

The sisters gave them cuttings from the tree. These they planted during the last breath of Moon, each offering a prayer to Lono, the god of growing things.

In the months that followed, Rustling Leaf tried to find a way to make cloth of the strange bark.

She beat strips of it on a stone with a wooden club; only shreds were left. Remembering her father's last words, she soaked the strips in water and then beat; slowly they grew wider. She beat several strips together; they formed one piece of wide bark cloth.

Now she had tapa, but it was not smooth enough. She tried beating the bark on a poi pounding board instead of on stone. The tapa took on a smooth, shining finish. It was ready to be made into warm clothing or, by fastening layers together, into bed covers.

The pounding board was made of a hardwood log which gave out a deep booming sound as the sisters worked. Whenever the village women heard it, they came and watched. They were eager to learn to make the wonderful bark cloth, but had to wait for their own bark. Their cuttings were green and strong but growing slowly in the usual way of trees, not overnight as had the miraculous parent tree.

The smooth gleaming tapa tempted Gifted Worker to decorate it. She made colors from roots and nuts. She made designs: first with a carved wooden beater; later with a carved bamboo stamp. She dipped the stamp into the dye bowl and pressed it on the tapa.

When finally the mulberry shoots grew large enough, the women came with strips of their own bark. The daughters of Maikoha taught them how to beat and stamp tapa. More and more women came to learn, and to ask for cuttings from the tree of The Hairy One. On clear warm days they worked outdoors, but when the weather turned cold or wet they had to stop.

The villagers, now clothed in warm bark cloth, remembered that it was Maikoha who had given it to them—from his very body. They offered thanks and praise to him and to his daughters also. They said of tapa, "It is clearer than the light of the moon; whiter than snow upon the mountains." They decided to set aside a sacred place to honor Maikoha and his daughters—a place for teaching, and for the making of tapa.

There was much to do: a large, grass house to build; a drying yard to fence in; stone and wooden anvils to make; wooden clubs, beaters, and bamboo stamps to carve; dyes to prepare. The image-maker set to work on an image of Maikoha.

When the Place-of-Tapa-Making was finished, the day came for the ceremonies. The people bathed, dressed in fresh tapa, and put on leis of fragrant maile vine. Everyone gathered with offerings of fruit and vegetables wrapped in pieces of newly made tapa.

Rustling Leaf and Gifted Worker were asked to take places at the head of the procession. They, too, carried offerings. All waited silently.

From a distance came the sound of the ceremonial drum. Nearer and nearer it sounded. The drummer came in sight and behind him a bearer, carrying the image of Maikoha on a tall pole.

Maikoha himself seemed to move toward the waiting people. Pearl-shell eyes looked down, and the mouth lined with small white shark's teeth smiled. The head, woven of vine roots and covered with rare red feathers, nodded gently. The strands of gray hair swayed in the breeze.

Maikoha's daughters watched as in a trance.

The image-bearer took his place in front of them, and the procession moved to the slow, stately beat of the drum.

Through the village, past the house of Maikoha and the rushing stream, to the Place-of-Tapa-Making, went the procession. There a wise man, or kahuna, dressed in white tapa, stood before a small shrine. The people knelt on the ground, Maikoha's image was set in place, the kahuna gave a chant.

Rustling Leaf and Gifted Worker placed their offerings before the image: a mulberry shoot and a tapa-beater, a dye bowl and a bamboo stamp. The villagers then placed their offerings.

The imu, baking since early morning, was opened and portions of steaming food were placed before the image. The kahuna gave his final chant:

"It is finished,
The Place-of-Tapa-Making!
O Maikoha, god of the mulberry tree,
O Maikoha, god of the beaten thing,
Here is a home for you;
Come down and live.
Here is an offering;
Come down and eat."

Then there was a great feast and the joyful singing of meles and the dancing of hulas.

MAUI TRAPS SUN

On the Wailuku River, not far from Rainbow Falls, lived the half-god, Maui. His mother, the goddess Hina, lived behind the falls in the Cave-of-Mists. In those times the days were short, but Maui found a way to lengthen them . . . .

MAUI WAS A YOUNG MAN of strength and courage. He had a magic club, a magic spear, and a magic canoe paddle, all given to him by his grandmother. In addition to these, he had special powers because he was the son of a goddess. He was very fond of his mother, Hina, and visited her nearly every day;

60

for his stepfather, Aikanaka-the-Wanderer, was often away from home.

The goddess Hina was known throughout the islands for her beauty and for the fine bark cloth she made. From the time Sun came through the eastern gate until he went through the western gate, Hina worked at her tapa. She gathered the bark herself from mulberry trees. She brought sea water in which to soak it. She pounded the wet bark on her tapa log.

One time when Maui was watching her, he said, "You spend all your days making tapa!"

Hina laid aside her wooden beater, smiling in a sad way. "For those who make tapa, the day is never long enough. This piece is ready to dry but already Sun turns toward the west. My tapa will still be damp when Evening Star hangs in the sky."

"This is Sun's fault. He travels too swiftly. I shall find him and tell him so!"

"O Maui, Sun is a god!"

"We are gods, too," Maui said.

"But small ones, with small power. And you are but a half-god," his mother reminded him. "Sun has great powers. No one has ever gone close to him and lived!"

"Then I shall be the first!" Maui boasted. "I shall catch Sun and make him promise to go more slowly."

Hina warned, "Take your magic club and paddle. You will surely need all the power you have."

First, Maui made snares. He gathered coconut fiber and twisted eight strong cords. At the end of each he tied a noose.

Then, as Evening Star appeared in the sky, he coiled his snares in his canoe, laid his magic club beside them, and picked up his magic paddle. One stroke carried him down the river, a second stroke to the island where Sun made his home in the crater of a dead volcano.

Maui left his canoe, took his eight snares and his magic club, and started up to House-of-Sun.

Swiftly he climbed the grassy slope. Slowly he climbed the steep side of the volcano. At the top, in the crater, Sun lay fast asleep under a blanket of clouds. Silently, Maui laid his snares. Then he hid behind a lava rock and slept through the night.

Before daybreak, Maui woke. Clouds were just beginning to roll out of the crater. Soon over its rim came Sun's longest leg, his first glittering ray of sunrise. Down the slope it came and into the center of Maui's snare it stepped.

Maui drew the cord tight and fastened it to the rock.

"What is this?" roared Sun.

"You are my prisoner," said Maui.

"Let me go at once!" Sun commanded. "I have a long journey to make."

"You will journey nowhere until you promise to travel more slowly," said Maui.

"I go swiftly so my night's rest will be longer. Why should I promise such a thing?" Sun demanded.

Maui picked up his magic club before he answered. "Because my mother Hina needs more time to dry her tapas."

"Tapas! I have no time for such things!"

Maui said no more. He swung his magic club against Sun's longest leg, breaking off a piece.

Sun screamed in pain and anger. He scrambled to get three more legs over the rim of the crater. But Maui had laid his snares

wisely, and each leg was caught fast. Sun thrashed about, blowing his fiery breath. Maui backed off and tied the three cords fast.

Four legs crawled over the crater's rim. Four more legs were caught. Now Sun was frightened. The more he struggled, the tighter the nooses became. One leg was broken and seven more tied fast. He began to bluster.

"You dare not kill me! Without my light, plants and trees would die! Without plants, your people would die!"

Maui looked up from the cord he was tying. "Sun, let us bargain. Promise to travel more slowly for part of the time and I shall let you go."

"Ae. I promise," said Sun crossly.

With his magic club, Maui broke the cords. Sun hurried off across the sky, and Maui paddled back with the good news for Hina.

After that, for part of each year, Sun traveled at his usual speed. Days were short and darkness came early. But the rest of the year, Sun traveled more slowly. Then the days were long and filled with sunshine, and Hina was able to dry her tapas.

Sun kept his promise. If there were times when he wanted to hurry, his broken ray reminded him of the strength and courage of the young half-god, Maui.

The MONSTER MO-O

The home of a goddess, the colors of a tapa, the body of a monster mo-o, a boiling pool—all are to be found in the Wailuku River . . . .

IT WAS THE TIME of hot weather and sudden showers. Near the Cave-of-Mists, Hina, the beautiful goddess, was printing designs on her tapa. Now that Sun gave her longer days she was happy and sang at her work.

She dipped her carved bamboo stamp into the stone bowl of rich red dye, tapped it to remove any drops, then pressed it firmly

65

on the bark cloth. On and on she went. Dip...tap...press. Dip...
tap...press. Each time, her stamp moved to the right. Each time,
the design grew.

Hina glanced up and saw dark clouds clinging to the mountain,
and worked faster. Something black and scaly on the river bank
was watching her, but she did not see it. She saw her son, Maui,
in his canoe and waved as he glided out into the bay. Fish were
running and he was heading for the deep-water fishing ground.

A spatter of rain struck. Quickly Hina gathered up her tapa,
stamps, and dye bowl and carried them into her cave behind Rainbow Falls.

On the river bank, the scaly black thing moved out into the open.
It was Kuna, the mo-o, who lived far up the river in a dark cave.
His natural form was that of an ugly monstrous lizard.

Hina's great beauty attracted him, and he came down the
river often to see her. The goddess felt no liking for him, and
this made Kuna very angry. He sometimes lashed the river with
his tail and sent torrents of water over the falls to torment her. At
other times he rolled great logs and boulders down the stream.
But Hina's cave was strong, and she had her son to protect her.
Kuna, knowing of Maui's great strength and special powers,
never dared to come around when he was near. But today he
had seen Maui leave.

The mo-o's heavy-lidded eyes gleamed. He had made up his
mind to destroy Hina this time. He sent a huge rock crashing
into the river just below the falls, blocking the rushing water.
Dammed up, the water rose higher and higher until it flooded
Hina's cave.

Hina snatched up a big sheet of tapa she used as a sleeping-

cover and ran outside. A few yards away she saw Kuna watching her and looked for a way of escape.

But Hina did not look into the sky. If she had, she might have seen a small Cloud climbing higher and higher, and taking on an odd shape. Maui had placed this Cloudlet to watch over his mother while he was fishing and had ordered it to signal him in this way if any danger threatened her. Although Maui had no power over the great Cloud Goddesses, he could control one of the child Clouds.

Hina tried to climb up the muddy river bank but slipped back. The mo-o came slithering closer. Hina was caught between the slippery banks, the raging river, and the monster. If she could reach the other side...

She looked at the tapa across her arm. The rain had dampened the cloth and made its design run in a rainbow of color, but the tapa was still strong. She scooped up a stone, tied it in one end of the tapa, and threw that end across the river. Using her goddess power, Hina stretched the cloth until it caught in the branches of a large tree. She pulled the end to test it. The tapa held fast.

Overhead, Cloudlet climbed higher, then floated, then was still.

Kuna was close behind Hina now. She held the tapa tightly and swung across the river, high into the tree.

Kuna plunged into the river, clawing at the tapa. Unable to reach Hina, now safe in the tree, he gave a roar of rage.

From down the river came a mightier roar than Kuna's. It was Maui, returning in answer to Cloudlet's signal. He saw Kuna's rock damming up the river and sprang from his canoe. With his magic club he split the rock in two. The trapped waters rushed on their way to the sea.

Kuna, when he heard Maui's cry, turned and crawled upstream along the bank above the falls. Maui saw Hina safe in the tree, snatched up his magic spear, and ran after the mo-o.

Maui saw him disappear into a dark cave and hurled his magic spear into the blackness. But in his anger he failed to take careful aim and missed. His spear thudded into the lava wall and hung there, quivering.

While Maui was pulling it free, the mo-o escaped and fled up the river, hunting for another spot to hide. He found a deep pool and hid in the murky water on the bottom.

This did not stop Maui. He asked the volcano goddess for help, and she gave it to him. Down the mountainside fiery chunks of lava rock came bounding. Into the river they went, turning the pool into a boiling pot and driving Kuna from the bottom. As the mo-o tried to clamber up the bank Maui threw his spear again, and this time he did not miss. His spear killed Kuna, and the boiling water swept his ugly body over Rainbow Falls to the rocks below.

There the mo-o lies today—the long black island known as Kuna. The currents of the Wailuku River surge about him. The waters of Rainbow Falls drum upon his back. The rains of every storm beat upon the monster mo-o who tried to kill the lovely goddess, Hina. Up the river the boiling pool still bubbles and swirls, and over the Cave-of-Mists Hina's rainbow tapa hangs, shimmering in the sun.

CALABASH OF THE WINDS

The winds of Hawaii are many and each has its name. Misty Wind, Smoky Wind, Dusty Wind, Stormy Wind, winds from North, South, East, and West—all are held fast in two great calabashes ....

IT WAS THE MONTH of two minds. The weather turned warm, then cool, and Maui felt restless. He decided to make a kite.

For the frame and crossbars he chose fine hau wood. It was strong but light in weight. For the covering he took one of his mother Hina's largest, strongest tapas. For the cord he cut great lengths of olona shrub and twisted the fibers. When the kite was finished it was forty-five feet across and seventy-five feet long. No one had ever seen such a kite!

There was no wind to fly it. So Maui asked two of his friends to help him carry it to Cave-of-the-Winds. As the great kite passed by, women left their tapa boards to watch; men left their digging sticks in the taro fields and followed.

At Cave-of-the-Winds Maui saw Keeper-of-the-Winds inside and called a greeting. The old man came out, blinking in the sunlight.

Maui said, "O Keeper-of-the-Winds, I have need of your breezes to fly my kite."

"It is truly a wonderful kite. Let us try it out," said the keeper.

He went inside the cave and brought out a small gourd covered with a lid.

"This calabash is Ipu Iki," he said. "It holds the gentle breezes."

They moved to a clearing, and softly Maui began chanting his kite song.

"O Wind, Soft Wind of Hilo,
Wind from the calabash of everlasting winds,
Come from Ipu Iki.
O Wind, Soft Wind of Hilo,
Come gently, come with mildness."

Keeper-of-the-Winds tipped the lid of Ipu Iki a little way, saying, "Have a care, now!"

Soft Wind of Hilo drifted out. Maui held the cord, and his friends raised the great kite. The wind could barely lift it.

Maui let out the cord and chanted,

"O Wind, Misty Wind of Waimea,
Hasten and come to me."

Keeper-of-the-Winds opened the lid a little more. Misty Wind swept out, sending the kite sailing over the treetops. Maui ran with the cord, calling, "More!"

"More! Give him more wind!" cried his friends.

"Yes, more!" the watching people shouted. "Give him all the winds in Ipu Iki!"

By this time, Keeper-of-the-Winds was as excited as the others. He scooped the lid off the small calabash and turned it upside down, as Maui chanted,

> "Dusty Wind of Puna,
> Smoky Wind of Kilauea,
> Hasten and come to me."

Dusty Wind and Smoky Wind rushed out, sending the great kite higher and higher, soaring like a sea bird out over the sea.

As the small calabash emptied, the kite began to fall. Maui quickly reeled in the cord, and his friends caught the kite as it came down. The watchers cheered.

"When will you fly it again?" they asked.

"Tomorrow, if the weather is clear," Maui replied.

Everyone went home. Keeper-of-the-Winds called his breezes back into Ipu Iki and popped the lid on.

Next morning Maui and his friends again brought the kite.

To Keeper-of-the-Winds he said, "Today is another day. A day to call the winds from your large calabash."

"The winds in Ipu Nui are not for kite-flying. They are as mighty as the gods. Do not be foolish, Maui." The old man spoke sternly.

"But I have great strength, and godly power," Maui answered, "I am not afraid."

He chanted,   "O winds, mighty as the gods,
.   Winds from the calabash of everlasting winds,
                Come from Ipu Nui!
                Strong wind from the east,
                Swirling wind from the north,
                Hasten and come to me!"

Inside the cave, the winds in the large calabash began to boil and churn, moaning and wailing as they struggled to get free. The keeper ran inside and brought out Ipu Nui, fighting to keep it covered. The lid leaped and clattered in his hands. East Wind swept out, snatched the kite, and blew it upward. Maui laughed and gripped the cord firmly.

North Wind burst out of Ipu Nui and sent the kite spinning. Laughing, Maui let the cord out. He was enjoying his battle with the winds. The keeper pressed down on the lid, but a gust from West Wind knocked it from his hands and rushed out. Then South Wind roared out of the calabash and went screaming and howling after the kite.

It tossed and tugged high above the treetops. Maui braced his feet and hung onto the cord, which throbbed in his hand. The sky grew dark. The great kite disappeared in a murky cloud bank.

Maui saw that he had reached the end of the cord, and called,
                "O winds, mighty as the gods,
                Return to Ipu Nui!"
But the winds were gone beyond Maui's call. Ipu Nui rolled from the hands of its keeper.

Maui tried to bring in his kite. A shudder ran down the cord. A shudder...a tug...and he went staggering backward, grasping an empty stick. Away went his kite! Over the river, over the tree-

tops, over the crater of the volcano. The winds had won.

Howling winds and driving rain swept the island. Everyone rushed home.

"Ipu Nui!" cried Keeper-of-the-Winds. "Bring me Ipu Nui!"

Maui found the calabash, and the keeper took it into the cave. He worked more than an hour coaxing the stubborn winds back. By that time every sheet of tapa set out to dry had been blown away, every taro field washed out.

After the storm, people would have nothing to do with Maui. Even Keeper-of-the-Winds shut himself in his cave and refused to answer his call. Maui grew more and more restless. To pass the time, he made a small kite and flew it near home. One day he noticed a pattern to the winds. He tied the kite to a rock and studied its movements for many days. The time came when he knew which winds brought dry, clear weather and which brought rain.

So one day when he saw a neighbor setting out for a distant taro patch, he warned him that a shower was coming. The man scowled and went on. Within an hour he came plodding back through a rain. Another day Maui warned a fisherman that a storm was on its way. The man paid no attention. He was swept from the rocks by angry waves and nearly drowned.

The news of Maui's weather kite spread. Soon his neighbors began to depend upon it. Would it be a good day to launch a canoe? To work the taro patch? Fish? Dry tapas?

After many months, people stopped calling him Maui-the-kite-flyer-who-brought-the-great-storm. They called him Maui-whose-kite-foretells-the-weather. Keeper-of-the-Winds became friendly. And never again did Maui call for special winds from Ipu Iki or Ipu Nui.

THE WOMAN IN MOON

Aikanaka wandered to far places. Never did he think that Hina, his wife, would journey to a place where he could not go . . . .

HINA'S HUSBAND, Aikanaka-the-Wanderer, was home again. The goddess should have been happy. She was not. She was happier living alone, with her son Maui coming often to visit. When Aikanaka stayed home with her, Maui usually went off adventuring.

Aikanaka on his travels was a bold hunter and fearless warrior.

Aikanaka at home was a teller of tall tales and a husband hard to please.

He wanted new loincloths and shoulder capes of finest tapa. He wanted good foods, baked in the imu. He wanted tasty poi, pounded from his own wet-land taro. He wanted fresh spring water to drink.

But where was Aikanaka when fresh bark was needed for tapa-making? When a wild pig or fat fish was needed for the imu? When the taro needed pounding into poi? When the water gourds needed filling?

Aia! Then Aikanka was busy, telling of the wild black boar that had charged him in the upland forest. Telling of the ugly giant squid that had caught his canoe and held it fast. Telling of the fierce green-eyed shark he had ridden from deep water to shallow, then killed. Telling of the savage one-eyed warrior who had come at him with a shark-tooth club.

Hina could not break in on such great tales; so she was left to do all the work alone. Morning Star found her building the fire in the earth oven. Sun at noon beat down upon her at her tapa-making. Sun at setting left her busy at her pounding board with poi pounder and water bowl. Evening Star lighted her path to the spring as she filled the large calabash with fresh water for the next day's needs.

From Sun rising to Sun setting, from the birth of Moon to the death of Moon, Hina worked and heard nothing but complaints. She did not even have Maui's visits, for he was away. She grew more and more weary. At last came a day when she could go on no longer.

Aikanaka, hungry for freshwater shrimp, had sent her with

her net to a distant stream. As Hina reached the water she saw a beautiful rainbow forming. Its misty path began in a grassy field and arched high into the sky. She looked at it with longing. She walked to the foot of the rainbow and set her foot upon it. It held firm. She took a step...another...and another. Then Hina tossed away the shrimp net and climbed the arching pathway. Up and up she went, away from her husband's tall tales, his endless complaints. On and on, through a world of mist, of coolness, of peace.

But soon the heat of Sun grew strong. Hina's head throbbed with pain. Her skin burned and blistered. She grew dizzy and stumbled and fell. Crawling, she tried to go on but her strength was gone. The goddess power she held on earth was useless here. Helplessly she slipped back down the rainbow path and fell to the earth beside her shrimp net.

All day Hina lay in the field where she had fallen. As Sun set and the roundness of Moon appeared in the sky, she felt her strength returning. Parched with thirst, burning with fever, she picked up her shrimp net and went home.

She met Aikanaka returning from the spring. His face was dark as a thundercloud. What had taken her so long? Where were the shrimps? Why had he been forced to fill the water calabash? That was woman's work!

Without a word the goddess took the brimming calabash from him. But instead of pouring the water into the smaller family gourds, she set the calabash to her lips. Thirstily she drained it.

Aikanaka gave a bellow of rage and raised his hand to strike her. As Hina drew back she saw, beyond him, a moon rainbow forming. She knew then what to do. Still without a word, she

turned and went into their cave. She came out carrying a water calabash and her favorite tapa board and beater.

Swiftly she walked to the foot of the rainbow that shimmered in the light of Moon. As her husband stared, Hina set her foot upon the gleaming trail and began to climb.

Aikanaka sprang after her. But Hina was already beyond his reach, and the misty path would not support his weight. With an angry cry he gave a mighty leap and caught Hina's ankle, twisting it.

She pulled free, gasping with pain. Limping, the goddess traveled the cool night path of the rainbow, up into the sky, toward beckoning Stars, out of sight.

There Hina lives to this day. When the sky is filled with soft white Clouds the goddess is spreading her tapa in the light of Sun to dry. When Thunder rumbles she is rolling away the heavy stones that keep her tapa sheets in place. When Lightning flashes she is shaking and folding her finished cloth.

On nights when Moon is full, if you look closely, you may see the beautiful goddess. There Hina sits resting, her twisted foot stretched out before her, her tapa board and beater at her side.

GLOSSARY

ORIGINALLY there was no written Hawaiian language, only a spoken one. Later, when a written language was needed, it was found that all the sounds could be expressed with twelve Roman letters: the five vowels and seven of the consonants.

The vowels each have a single sound:

a.....ah   e.....ay   i.....ee   o.....oh   u.....oo

The consonants have the same sounds as in English, and they are: h, k, l, m, n, p, w. Pronunciation follows two simple rules:

Every vowel is sounded: Hiiaka, Hee-ee-ah-kah.

Every syllable ends with a vowel: Ka-me-ha-me-ha, not
Kam-e-ham-e-ha.

ae (*ah*-ee), yes
aia (*ah*-ee-ah), behold, look
Aikanaka (*Ah*-ee-kah-*nah*-kah)
aloha (ah-*loh*-hah), greeting which can mean hello or goodbye
hau (*hah*-oo), a tree having strong, light-weight wood
Hiiaka (Hee-ee-*ah*-kah), goddess of lightning
Hilo (*Hee*-loh), a district on the island of Hawaii
Hina (*Hee*-nah), a goddess
Hopoe (Hoh-*poh*-ay)
hula (*hoo*-lah), traditional dance, originally sacred
humu-humu-nuku-nuku-a-puaa
    (*hoo*-moo-*hoo*-moo-*noo*-koo-*noo*-koo-ah-poo-*ah*-ah),
    small grunting fish with snout like a pig's

imu (*ee*-moo), earth oven in which foods were roasted
Ipu Iki (*Ee*-poo *Ee*-kee), small gourd
Ipu Nui (*Ee*-poo *Noo*-ee), large gourd
Ka-ehu (Kah-*ay*-hoo)
Kahana (Kah-*hah*-nah), a district on the island of Oahu
Kahoa (Kah-*hoh*-ah)
kahuna (kah-*hoo*-nah), wise man, priest, one who conducted
    sacred ceremonies
Kamapuaa (*Kah*-mah-poo-*ah*-ah)
Ka Moho (Kah *Moh*-hoh), god of steam
Kana (*Kah*-nah)
Kanaloa (*Kah*-nah-*loh*-ah), god of the sea; one of the four
    great gods
Kane (*Kah*-nay), god of creation; the greatest Hawaiian god
Kauai (Kah-oo-*ah*-ee), an island of the Hawaiian chain
Ka-ulu (Kah-*oo*-loo)
Ke Aka (Kay *Ah*-kah)
Kilauea (*Kee*-lah-oo-*ay*-ah), a volcanic crater on the
    island of Hawaii
koa (*koh*-ah), a tree whose wood is used especially for
    canoe-making
Kona (*Koh*-nah), a district on island of Hawaii
Ku (Koo), god of forests; one of the four great gods
Kuna (*Koo*-nah)
kupua (koo-*poo*-ah), half-god, half-man with supernatural
    powers, especially that of changing form
lehua (lay-*hoo*-ah), a tree with feathery red blossoms;
    grows in cooled lava flow areas
lei (lay), garland of flowers or leaves worn around neck or head
Lono (*Loh*-noh), god of growing things; one of the four
    great gods
Maikoha (Mah-ee-*koh*-hah)

maile (*mah*-ee-lay), a fragrant vine used for leis, especially in
  sacred ceremonies
malo (*mah*-loh), loincloth worn by early Hawaiian men and boys
Maui (*Mah*-oo-ee), half-god, half-man; also name of an island
  in the Hawaiian chain
Mauna Kea (*Mah*-oo-nah *Kay*-ah), White Mountain, a
  snow-capped mountain on the island of Hawaii
mele (*may*-lay), song or chant
mo-o (*moh*-oh), Hawaiian form of dragon; often resembled a
  monster lizard
Namaka (Nah-*mah*-kah), goddess of the sea
Niheu (Nee-*hay*-oo)
olona (oh-*loh*-nah), a plant used for cord and rope
Olopana (Oh-loh-*pah*-nah)
Oahu (Oh-*ah*-hoo), an island of the Hawaiian chain
pa-u (pah-*oo*), skirt worn by women of early Hawaii;
  sometimes a length of cloth wrapped about waist with
  end drawn up over one shoulder
Pele (*Pay*-lay), goddess of the volcano
poi (*poh*-ee), staple food of Hawaiians; made from taro root
  pounded with water to make thick paste
Poliahu (Poh-lee-*ah*-hoo), goddess of snow
Puna (*Poo*-nah), a dry desert area on island of Hawaii
tapa (*tah*-pah), [modern spelling of kapa] cloth made from bark
taro (*tah*-roh), [modern spelling of kalo] plant from whose
  bulbs poi is made; two varieties, wet-land and dry-land
Uli (*Oo*-lee), a goddess of sorcery
Wailuku (Wah-ee-*loo*-koo), a river in Hilo
Waimea (Wah-ee-*may*-ah), a foggy section of island of Hawaii
Waipio (Wah-ee-*pee*-oh), a deep valley on island of Hawaii
wiliwili (*wee*-lee-*wee*-lee), a tree having light-weight wood
  used for floats on outrigger canoes

bibLiogRApby

BEAMER, NONA K. *Hawaiiana Study Unit*. Dept. of Ed.: Hilo, Hawaii, 1964

BECKWITH, MARTHA W. *Kumulipo, A Hawaiian Creation Chant* (trans.). Univ. of Chicago Press, 1951; *Hawaiian Mythology*. Yale Univ. Press, 1940

BUCK, PETER H. *Arts and Crafts of Hawaii*. Bishop Museum Press: Honolulu, 1957

ELBERT & KEALA. *Conversational Hawaiian*. Univ. of Hawaii Press: Honolulu, 1961.

EMERSON, NATHANIEL B. *Pele and Hiiaka*. Honolulu Star Bulletin Press: Honolulu, 1915

FORNANDER, ABRAHAM. *An Account of the Polynesian Race*. 3 vols. London, 1878-1885; *Collection of Hawaiian Antiquities and Folklore*. Bishop Museum Press: Honolulu, 1916-1920

JUDD, PUKUI, STOKES. *Introduction to the Hawaiian Language*. Tongg Pub. Co.: Honolulu, 1945

LEIB, AMOS P. *Hawaiian Legends in English, An Annotated Bibliography*. Univ. of Hawaii Press: Honolulu, 1949

LUOMALA, KATHARINE. *Voices on the Wind, Polynesian Myths and Chants*. Bishop Museum Press: Honolulu, 1955

MACDONALD & HUBBARD. "Volcanoes of Hawaii National Park," *Hawaii Nature Notes*, Vol. IV, No. 2, May 1951. Hawaii Natural History Assoc.

MALO, DAVID. *Hawaiian Antiquities*. Bishop Museum Press: Honolulu, 1898, 1951

PUKUI & ELBERT. *English-Hawaiian Dictionary*. Univ. of Hawaii Press: Honolulu, 1964

RICE, WM. HYDE. *Hawaiian Legends*. Bishop Museum Press: Honolulu, 1923

TAYLOR, CLARICE B. *Hawaiian Almanac*. Tongg Pub. Co.: Honolulu, 1957

THRUM, THOMAS G. *More Hawaiian Folk Tales*. A. C. McClurg & Co.: Chicago, 1923

WESTERVELT, WM. D. *Hawaiian Legends of Ghosts and Ghost-Gods*. Chas. E. Tuttle Co.: Tokyo, 1915, 1963; *Hawaiian Legends of Old Honolulu*. ibid.; *Hawaiian Legends of Volcanoes*. ibid., 1916, 1963; *Legends of Maui, A Demi-God*. Hawaiian Gazette Co.: Honolulu, 1910